John Smith is NOT BORING!

My name is John Smith – the most boring name in the world. Dad says with a name like John Smith no one will EVER make fun of me. Mum says I'm "one in a MILLION". My sister says it makes me the most boring person in history. But do not judge a book by its cover. My life is ANYTHING but boring!

To Lottie-Lou, Daisy-Doo ... and Florence too!

First published in the UK in 2015 by Scholastic Children's Books
An imprint of Scholastic Ltd
Euston House, 24 Eversholt Street
London, NW1 1DB, UK
Registered office: Westfield Road, Southam, Warwickshire, CV47 0RA
SCHOLASTIC and associated logos are trademarks and/or registered
trademarks of Scholastic Inc.

Text copyright © Johnny Smith, 2015
Illustrations © Laura Ellen Anderson, 2015

The right of Johnny Smith and Laura Ellen Anderson to be identified as the
author and illustrator of this work respectively has been asserted by them.

ISBN 978 1407 15195 3

A CIP catalogue record for this book is available from the British Library.

Printed by CPI Group (UK) Ltd, Croydon, CR0 4YY
Papers used by Scholastic Children's Books are made from wood
grown in sustainable forests.

1 3 5 7 9 10 8 6 4 2

This is a work of fiction. Names, characters, places, incidents and
dialogues are products of the author's imagination or are used fictitiously.
Any resemblance to actual people, living or dead, events or locales is entirely
coincidental.

www.scholastic.co.uk

CHAPTER ONE

"Boring! Boring! Boring! Boring! Boring!"

"Why don't you go and play in your bedroom?" says Mum.

"Why don't you go and play in the garden?" says Dad.

"Why don't you go and play on the other side of the world?" says my big sister, Hayley.

The Smith family are all together. Mum's watching her favourite film, *Attack of the Mutant Death Chimps*; Dad's dozing

1

underneath a newspaper; Hayley and her boyfriend, Rufus, are curled up on the sofa touching toes; and Granddad is picking his dentures out of a block of toffee with a screwdriver.

"But I'm so bored," I repeat.

"Only boring people get bored," says Mum.

"And you should know," Hayley laughs.

Oh no, here we go again. Hayley's favourite subject. . .

"You're the most boring person in the world – with the most boring name in the world! I'm almost falling asleep just staring at your dreary little face."

"You do indeed have a very boring name," says Rufus. "Did you know there are nearly half a million John Smiths on the planet. . .?"

"But there's only ever been one Rufus Randall the Third," sighs Hayley.

"I think you'll find there've been at least three," I snort.

"Be quiet, vermin!" snaps Hayley.

Everyone goes back to watching the film. After a bit longer I pipe up: "Why *did* you call me John Smith, Dad?"

Dad drops his paper, looks at Mum anxiously, searching for an answer. "Because with a name like John Smith, nobody will ever make fun of you," he says.

Hayley begins to giggle.

"Why did you call Hayley Hayley?" I reply.

"We named her after Halley's Comet," says Mum, "because she's our bright little star."

"Aw," says Hayley, "sweet."

"I thought a comet was a long streak of gas," mutters Granddad.

I burst out laughing. "Good one, Granddad!"

Hayley looks at me, her eyes draining to ice.

"Let me tell you something about you, John Smith. You're nothing. You're no one. You're never going to be anybody. Why? Because you're John Smith. I'll say it again — in capitals. JOHN SMITH. I'll underline it too: <u>JOHN SMITH</u>! Are you getting the message? You are a complete nobody. As for me…" Hayley suddenly springs off the sofa and throws her arms in the air. "I was born to be a star!"

Tonight is curtain up on Hayley's big school show, and she's playing the lead role. I look at Rufus and pull a funny face. "She loves me really."

"No I don't, cross my heart and hope to die," says Hayley. "Haven't you got homework or something to fail at, you miserable little cockroach?"

Granddad farts.

Mum pretends there's a bee in the room.

Hayley moves to the door, dangling Rufus on her little finger. "If anybody needs me," she smiles, "I'll be starring in the school play."

"We've got front row tickets," says Mum.

"Break a leg," says Dad.

Hayley glides out of the house and down the garden path.

"If anybody needs me ... I'll be in my bedroom," I sigh.

CHAPTER TWO

I live in an ordinary little house which is sort of square and a bit yellow and a bit white round the edges and a bit brown on the top, and it's in the middle of a street with green bits and grey bits. You get the picture.

Apart from me and Mum and Dad and Hayley, we also live with Granddad. His name is John Smith too. As Hayley always says, my name is so common I'm not even the only John Smith in my own home.

But here's this thing you should know: I have this massive, massive, MASSIVE secret. I can travel into other worlds and go on amazing adventures. Granddad is an adventurer too. It's this big thing we share.

Granddad says we're members of something called the John Smith Club. He says you don't have to have a fancy name to have a big adventure – just because you sound like a NOBODY you might actually be a SOMEBODY. Granddad says if you see a John Smith in the street he'll have this BIG secret too.

I flop on the bed and think about my homework. I've got to write a story all about knights in shining armour.

I'd love to be a knight riding round the countryside, swishing my sword over my head, fighting off fire-breathing dragons! Talking of fire-breathing dragons, I wonder if knights have annoying big sisters too. And here's another thought: do you think knights fart inside their suits of armour? You have to admit, there are some interesting questions to be answered. I have to do a show and tell and right now I'm not showing or telling anything. I haven't got a single thing to share with my class. Come on, brain, THINK!

Then it hits me. If I want to be a knight in armour I CAN be a knight in armour. I can have this brilliant, amazing adventure AND get one up in class. I love it when a genius idea comes together.

I run out of my room and straight into Granddad shuffling out of the loo, a sheet of toilet paper flapping off his shoe.

"Granddad, I wanna go on an adventure! Can you help me?"

Granddad gives me a cheeky wink.

In the middle of Granddad's room is a battered old trunk covered with stickers of gladiators, spacemen and spies.

"You want to journey to faraway lands?" says Granddad, popping his head up from inside the trunk. "The world is your lobster! So what's the adventure going to be this time?"

"I want to wear a suit of armour. I want to

ride a horse. I want to win tournaments..."

"You want to be a knight in armour," chortles Granddad. "I was a knight in armour once..."

Granddad suddenly stops chortling and bites his lip. "On the other hand, you could choose a different adventure," he mutters. "We could send you somewhere just as exciting – the bottom of the ocean or the far reaches of outer space. All you have to do is say the word."

"But this could really help with my homework, Granddad," I protest. "I've got to write a story about knights in armour..."

Granddad nods and smiles. "Then a knight ye shall be..."

Inside the trunk are pirate hats, cowboy boots, spaceman suits ... and what's this? A knight's sword and shield!

"So what do you think?" says Granddad.

"It's one in the eye for my big sister," I

chortle, swiping my sword around the room. "If she could see me now..."

"Are you ready for the adventure of a lifetime?" says Granddad.

"I was born ready!" I beam, proudly.

Granddad goes to the bedroom door and turns to face me. "It's time to say the magic words..."

Holding my sword and shield, I take a deep breath and read the special words written on the trunk:

"Say it long, say it loud – I'm JOHN SMITH and I'm proud!"

Granddad throws the bedroom door wide open. "Go forth, John Smith ... knight of this realm!"

I can hear cheering and trumpets and horses' hooves!

"Have fun," chuckles Granddad. "And don't lose your head!"

CHAPTER THREE

Everyone is chanting my name...

"John Smith! John Smith! John Smith!"

I'm riding into a castle on a huge black horse. The bells in the tower are ringing out; the crowds are cheering.

Someone shouts out, "John Smith has come to save us!"

Someone else shouts out, "All hail John Smith!"

And then someone says, "He is the greatest

name in the land!"

What can I say? I like the sound of this! I give the crowd a big wave and they all cheer again.

"You are most popular, sire!" says a boy who's holding my horse as he leads me into the courtyard. "John Smith is such an amazing and wonderful name. I've never heard anything like it."

"It's true it is a very rare name," I reply. "Down my way I'm one of a kind."

"I am Oswald Periwinkle," says the boy. "I know what you're thinking. You're thinking, what a very common name. When I asked my father why he called me Oswald Periwinkle, he said—"

"Because with a name like that, no one will ever make fun of you?" I interrupt.

Oswald looks at me and gasps. "You can read my mind, John Smith. It's true what they say – you are touched by greatness!"

Oswald holds his hand out to help me off the horse.

"Come with me. The Queen is waiting in her castle." He pats me on the shoulder and smiles. "You can call me Ossie."

I follow Ossie into the castle, through a massive hall with pictures of old kings and queens on the walls and past the heralds blowing their trumpets.

A messenger shouts out, "All kneel for Her Majesty, the Queen!"

At the top of the hall the Queen sits on a shiny gold throne wearing a shiny gold crown.

I kneel before her.

Standing next to the Queen is a really scary man with an axe who looks just like my headmaster. "Watch out for him," whispers

Ossie. "That's the Queen's executioner, Woodworm!"

The Queen rises to her feet and looks at me. Everyone listens very closely.

"John Smith, your name is legend around these parts. And such an unusual name..." says the Queen.

The crowd all nod their heads.

"You are probably wondering why we have sent for you."

"Speak, Your Queenliness," I reply.

"We have a big problem," says the Queen. "Ivan the Horrible is going to wreak havoc on our castle, causing much mayhem and misery. This is why we have sent for you, John Smith! We want you to do battle with Ivan the Horrible and we really want you to try your hardest to KILL him!"

"They don't call me John Smith for nothing, Your Majesty!" I reply. "I'll take care of your little problem."

"Three cheers for John Smith!" someone shouts out.

And everyone cheers, including the horses.

The Queen slumps in her throne and scratches her cheek. "Haven't I seen you somewhere before?" she says.

"Oh no, Your Majesty, there is only one of me!" I laugh. Which of course is a completely enormous fib; there are millions of me!

"Very well, then. Eat, drink and be merry," she chuckles. "For very soon you will probably be dead."

CHAPTER FOUR

I do not like the sound of this! The eating bit, the drinking bit, the being merry bit — that all sounds ace. But the being dead very soon bit scares the pants off me! Still, I must put on a brave face.

I stride out of the castle. The heralds blow their trumpets and everyone is nudging each other and gawping at me.

"You don't seem very frightened," says Ossie. "After all, you're going to fight Ivan the Horrible, and he's a real rotten meanie!"

"Frightened?" I scoff. "I don't know the meaning of the word."

"It means terrified, scared, speechless..." says Ossie.

We walk back into the courtyard where my horse is waiting. Ossie gives me the reins.

"What a magnificent beast!" says Ossie, patting the horse on the neck. "I suppose you travel far and wide on your trusty steed?"

"Oh yes," I chortle, "up and down the country riding my fine four-legged friend."

The truth is that I've never seen this horse before in my life.

I climb on to the horse and wave to the crowd. Then I lift my sword over my head and try to swing it around a bit; they seem to like that sort of thing. The sword is so heavy I nearly backflip off the horse.

We trot across the courtyard. I take the cheers from the crowd again, feeling generally marvellous.

"Does your horse have a name?" asks Ossie.

"Um, yes, she's called Daisy!" I reply.

The horse snorts.

I lean over and pat the horse on the side of the neck. "We're a right regular team, aren't we, Daisy? We go together like sausage and mustard, bacon and eggs, cheese and onnniiiioooooooonnnnnn..."

Suddenly the horse shoots off really fast.

I'm bouncing about in the saddle, trying to hold on to the reins. The crowd gasp and cheer as I charge round the courtyard, desperately clinging on, my sword and shield clattering and battering around me. My suit of armour is clanking all over the place, my

visor is rattling up and down in front of
my face and my helmet is bashing all over
my head!

"STOPPPPPP!!!!"

The horse comes to a
sudden stop and throws
me clean over her
head. I plunge face
down in a trough
of pig swill.

I roll over,
wipe the slime
from my eyes
and look at the
crowd.

They are all staring at me with their mouths wide open. This is NOT what they were expecting. I straighten my helmet, clean myself off and stagger back to my horse.

"And there's plenty more where that came from!" I announce, pretending I meant to do it all along.

The horse looks at me and blows two jets of hot air out of her nostrils, then does a massive dump on the cobblestones.

"Better out than in," I say.

"Follow me," says Ossie. "I'll take you to my home."

"Rightio," I grunt.

I pull myself on to the horse again.

"You're facing the wrong way," says Ossie.

"That's right," I reply, bluffing. "I'd like it to be a surprise!"

I hope Ossie believes me because I'm

actually making all this up as I go along.

Ossie tells me all about the Queen. He says she has been heartbroken since her red ruby was stolen and if she ever finds the thief she'll make him pay! Ossie says the Queen's executioner, Woodworm, will chop his head off and use it as a football.

"That's bound to hurt," I laugh.

"Which bit?" says Ossie. "Getting your head chopped off or having it used as a football?"

"Both," I gulp.

As we cross the courtyard, Ossie shows me a massive comic strip on the wall, which he says is called a tapestry. It's like a big carpet with pictures of lots and lots of people. I can see Ossie, the Queen, Woodworm the executioner and lots of other folk I don't recognize.

"It was done a while back," says Ossie. "I completely forgot to clean my teeth and

brush my hair. Mum went mad!"

I really like Ossie. I think we're going to be friends.

"OK" says Ossie, "this is where I live!"

Ossie's house is a bit black and a bit white with lots of little hanging baskets on the porch, a blackboard on a stand offering something called "traditional fayre" and lots of barrels outside the front door.

"Ye Olde Inn?" I say, reading the sign by the door. What sort of place is this? And why have they written *Old* with an *e*?

"My dad runs the local pub," says Ossie.

The front door opens and a little man with rosy red cheeks and a tea towel over his arm comes running out to greet us.

"Dad, this is the great John Smith," says Ossie. "He's come to save us!"

"Oh, thank ye, sir," says Ossie's dad, shaking me by the hand. "Thank ye, thank

ye, a thousand thank ye's..."

A rosy-cheeked lady in a yellow apron bustles out of the door.

Ossie nudges me. "You'll love my mum."

"An honour to meet you, young man!" says Ossie's mum. She wipes her hand on her apron and sticks it out. "Please excuse me, I've just been scattering cow dung on my turnips."

I shake her hand carefully.

"Sorry, wrong hand," she giggles. "Come inside, John Smith, and settle yourself down. You must be starving."

I tie Daisy up and follow Ossie and his mum and dad inside.

CHAPTER FIVE

We sit at the kitchen table and
Ossie's mum gives me turnip
cake and turnip tea.
Turnips! Yucky! Worse
than sprouts!

"We've got turnip biscuits
as well if you're not a
big fan of turnip cake?"
she chuckles.

"You haven't got

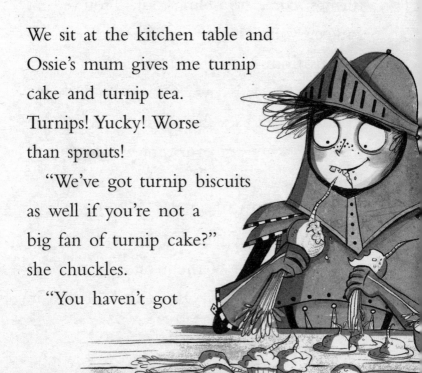

a cheese toastie, have you?" I mumble. I realize I'm really hungry.

"We could do you a turnip toastie," says Ossie's dad.

"No, no, this is lovely," I mumble, chewing lumps of raw turnip.

"Well, there's plenty more where that came from," says Ossie's mum as she opens the pantry door and about half a million turnips come tumbling out. "You've got to keep your strength up if you're going to save us from Ivan the Horrible."

"So tell us," says Ossie's dad, "what stunning victories have you notched up then, you know, in your time as a legendary knight."

I don't want to let them down, so I have to make up some tales. "Well – dragons, I've seen one or two of them off..."

"A dragon?" says Ossie's dad. "I like it.

What was it then, a fire-breathing beast with red eyes, green scales and vicious claws?"

"Yes," I reply, "that's the sort of thing."

"Have a name, did it, this dragon?" says Ossie's mum.

I cough a little as I try to come up with a name.

"This one was called Hayley," I nod.

Ossie looks at me, a little disappointed.

"Hayley the Dragon? What kind of a name is that?" says Ossie's dad. "I was expecting something like Flames of Fury or The Scorcher!"

"Don't judge a book by its cover," I reply. "I have looked into Hayley's eyes close up and she is a monster and a half!"

"And how did you defeat this dragon called Hayley?" says Ossie's mum.

"I fed her a diet of baked beans and fizzy

drink until she barfed and burped at the same time and blew herself to smithereens!" I laugh.

"What a cunning ploy," says Ossie, before adding, "What are baked beans?"

"And what's fizzy drink?" asks Ossie's mum.

"You know, a special brew with lots of bubbles like lemonade or orangeade."

"I know exactly what you mean," says Ossie's mum. "We call ours turnipade."

"So you're going to defeat Ivan the Horrible, are you?" says Ossie's dad, going back to the reason why I'm here.

"The scallywag steals our food," says Ossie's mum. "I'm down to my last ten thousand turnips!"

"Have no fear, John Smith is here!" I beam. "I will see him off!"

"But what about his army?" says Ossie's mum. "That gang of bloodthirsty brigands and villains with their axes, swords, pots of boiling pitch, spears, chains and spikes!"

"He's got an army?" I mutter. "Nobody said anything about an army!"

"A terrible, murderous crew they are," says Ossie's dad. "There's Bruno the Bone Breaker, Thor the Eyeball Sucker, and worst of all ... Terry the Toe Tickler!"

"Then they reckoned without John Smith," I announce. "I'll show them exactly who they're dealing with! I'll have the lot of them for breakfast!"

"You'll have them for breakfast?" gasps Ossie. "Eurgh! That sounds horrible."

"Another slice of turnip cake?" says Ossie's mum. "All you have to do is say the magic word."

"Go on," says Ossie's dad, "it'll put hair on your chest..."

Ossie's mum slices a quarter of the turnip

cake on to my plate.

"So what's the BIG PLAN?" asks Ossie's dad.

I pace around the room, weighing up the situation. Then I stop dramatically and address them. "I think I have the answer!"

Ossie's mum and dad cheer.

"What is it?" asks Ossie. "What? WHAT?"

"What we need ... is a BIG PLAN!"

"I just said that," says Ossie's dad.

"Is that the best you've got?" says Ossie's mum.

"I could always use my bow and arrow," says Ossie.

"One bow and arrow against a whole army," I sigh. "They'll make mincemeat of us!"

Suddenly I hear a noise in the street. I rush to the window, my sword at the ready.

"What's that terrible racket?" I gasp. "It

sounds like a honking cat. It's putting me off thinking up my big plan!"

I see someone in the middle of the courtyard, skipping round in circles.

"That is Perkin the Pied Piper," says Ossie. "He walks round the castle grounds playing his penny whistle."

"It's a horrible sound," I groan. "It's giving

me a headache!"

"He's not a very good piper," says Ossie.

"He's complete manure!" says Ossie's dad. "I've heard smarter tunes from an armpit fart!"

"Wait. So, if you've got a pied piper ... you've got mice?" I ask, an idea forming in my mind.

"Thousands of the little critters," says Ossie's dad.

"Millions," says Ossie's mum.

"They scurry all over the castle," says Ossie. "They're a right proper pest."

"You've got a really queer look on your face, John Smith," says Ossie's mum.

"These mice might be the answer to our problems," I smile.

I go back to the kitchen table and pick up my shield and helmet.

"I want everyone in the castle courtyard in five minutes!"

CHAPTER SIX

"Good friends, people of this fair castle – lend me your cheese!"

"What do you want with our cheese?" someone in the crowd shouts out.

"I got some cheese you can have," says a beggar in rags.

He scrapes a knob of green, creamy goo from underneath his toenail. "That's pure toe cheese," he chuckles. "The slightest whiff could knock out an entire army."

He's right. It smells worse than Hayley's dirty washing basket!

"Does anyone have any cheese?" I shout, gasping and coughing from the disgustingly smelly smell. "Just the teensiest, weensiest crumb?"

The crowd mutter and mumble and shake their heads.

"You're telling me this is a castle without cheese?" I gasp. "That is impossible. Impossible! Life without cheese is not worth living. You can grate it or slice it or melt it..."

I close my eyes and lose myself in a cheesy daydream.

"Take the cheese toastie – dribbling with

promise, the cheese dangling round your lips like dairy-flavoured rubber bands. Oh, I can taste it now, give me more … GIVE ME MORE!"

When I open my eyes, everyone is staring at me, blinking.

"He's a nutcase," someone shouts.

"Afternoon," says a cheery voice behind us.

"This is our local cheesesmith, Egbert," says Ossie.

"I heard you were asking for cheese," says Egbert. "Frankly, I'm delighted to get rid of the stuff, so here you go…."

Egbert dumps a huge wodge of cheese on the cobblestones.

"Wow. That is cheese to the power of a million!" I gulp.

"Delicious," says Ossie. "I'm starving!"

"This cheese is not for eating," I announce. "This cheese is battle cheese!"

"Battle cheese?" says Ossie.

"Oh yes," I smile. "We're going to build the world's greatest mousetrap!"

There's lots of tutting, sighing and general shaking of heads.

"The mice won't fall for this," says Perkin the Pied Piper. "They're not stupid, you know. They're mice. Call yourself a knight of the realm? I'll tell you what I think of this idea."

Perkin puts his pipe up his bottom and blows a loud PARP!

"Look!" says Ossie.

A little furry army scamper across the cobblestones.

"You did it, Perkin!" I cheer.

"Mice," says the Pied Piper. "Hundreds of mice!"

"Thousands of mice," says Egbert.

"Let the mice approach the cheese!" I whisper.

The mice scurry across the cobblestones, their whiskers twitching, their noses working furiously, following the big old cheesy stench.

"It's working," says Ossie, digging me in the ribs. "The mice are taking the bait."

They approach the cheese from all sides and nibble away.

"What do we do now?" asks Ossie's dad.

"Hats at the ready," I murmur. "Let Operation Scoop the Little Critters begin!"

We race across the courtyard, plucking the mice into our pockets, plopping them under our hats, tucking them down our trousers.

"Hold on a minute," says Egbert the Cheesesmith. "What have these mice got to do with Ivan the Horrible?"

I open my mouth to tell them my big plan when the heralds blow their trumpets.

The messenger appears on the scene and announces, "All kneel for Her Majesty, the Queen..."

Chapter Seven

The Queen walks into the courtyard with Woodworm, her scary executioner.

"John Smith," says the Queen, "are you preparing yourself for the battle you must fight?"

"Oh yes, Your Maj," I reply.

The Queen looks at me and smiles. "Cheeky little terrier, aren't you? Ivan the Horrible will be here very soon. He will lead his mighty army up the hill, charge over the drawbridge, smash down the castle gate and ransack the castle. And you are the only person who can stop him."

The Queen suddenly looks across the courtyard.

"That's a rather large lump of cheese," she says.

"We're rounding up the mice," says Perkin.

"Why are you rounding up the mice?" asks the Queen.

Perkin stares blankly ahead, blowing out a big breath. "You've got me there," he grunts.

"It's all part of my plan, Your Majesty," I say.

"You're using these mice to defeat the mighty Ivan and his band of bloodthirsty bandits?" says the Queen.

"If you're the great John Smith," sneers Woodworm, "why don't you ride into battle waving your sword over your head and kill

Ivan the Horrible in the traditional manner instead of resorting to death by mouse?"

Woodworm suddenly spins his axe over his head and throws it into the ground just in front of my feet. "You could use my axe!" he smirks.

Everyone turns and looks at me. That Woodworm is rotten, but he does have a point! If I'm such a brave and famous knight, why don't I do the knightly thing and put Ivan the Horrible to the sword?

"Well, John Smith?" says the Queen. "What do you have to say to that?"

"Well, Your Majesty…" I walk round in a little circle, trying to think of something really clever to say. "That is … uh … exactly what Ivan the Horrible would expect me to do."

Some people nod, but most of them just look a bit confused. I think I'll have to go for broke. "They would expect me – John

Smith – to do something – LIKE THIS!"

I pick up Woodworm's axe and spin it round over my head. "Charge into battle swinging my mighty axe!" I yell.

The axe accidentally slips out of my fingers and slices into one of the barrels outside Ye Olde Inn. A column of beer spews up in a big frothy fountain. Everyone claps. Clearly they think I meant to do this.

"But then again," I say, getting into my stride, "maybe Ivan the Horrible would expect me to do ... this!" I pull out my sword, stick it in the ground and spectacularly vault straight on to Daisy.

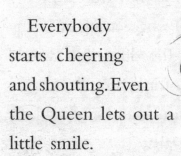

Everybody
starts cheering
and shouting. Even
the Queen lets out a
little smile.

Unfortunately,
Daisy has other ideas.
She bolts off around the courtyard. I bounce
around in the saddle, waving my sword.

"Look at him go!" they shout. "What an
extraordinary hero!"

Daisy runs past Ye Olde Inn. My sword accidentally cuts the hanging baskets. They drop on the Queen's heralds one by one.

The last and the biggest basket smashes over Woodworm's head, leaving him coughing and spluttering, spitting out soil.

The crowd are roaring and clapping wildly.

Daisy suddenly stops, but this time I'm one step ahead of her. As I fly free, I slip my feet into the bindings on the back of my shield and skid across the cobblestones. I ride the shield like a skateboard, flipping a trick up the side of a hay cart, somersaulting through the air and landing back at the Queen's feet. Everyone is cheering and clapping me on the back.

"That was quite a display," says the Queen.

"Wouldn't you agree, Mr Woodworm?"

Woodworm spits the final bits of mud out of his mouth and eyes me up. "It's certainly left a lasting impression on me, Your Majesty," he scowls.

The Queen looks at me quizzically.

"John Smith," she says.

"That's me, Your Majesty!" I flash the Queen my winning smile, the one I reserve for extra special occasions when I've been really naughty.

The Queen shakes her head and bites her lip, then lets out a really long sigh. "I've seen you somewhere before, haven't I?" she says. "I'm positive of it."

She turns to Woodworm. "Have you seen this boy somewhere before, Mr Woodworm?"

"I know a face when I see one," says the Queen's executioner.

"And the back of a head too," laughs the Queen.

The Queen drums her fingers, thinking, thinking...

"Wait a minute, wait a minute," she says. She bites her thumbnail, lost in thought. "It's just coming to me... John Smith... John Smith..." Her eyes narrow as if she's arriving at an important thought. Her face suddenly lights up, her eyes bulging like saucers.

"I have it," she gasps. "I know where I've seen you before!"

Suddenly, the messenger runs into the courtyard and announces: "Ivan the Horrible is at the castle gates!"

Everyone starts to run around screaming in a blind panic. The Queen fixes me with a stare and slowly nods.

"Well, John Smith," she says. "Kill this hideous villain!"

"Leave it with me, your Queenly Queenship," I reply.

Chapter Eight

Ivan the Horrible looks horribly nasty and really scary and he sits on the biggest horse ever, which looks horribly nasty and scary too! Ivan the Horrible obviously doesn't brush his hair or shave his chin or clean his teeth. I'll bet he's never even heard of flossing!

He rides into the castle ahead of his terrible army, clunking away in their suits of armour. Ossie points them out one by one.

"Bruno the Bone Breaker, Thor the Eyeball Sucker, Terry the Toe Tickler..." he gulps.

"And lots of other rotten-looking types," I reply.

Ivan's gang have got pikes and spikes and spears and swords and a massive wooden catapult on wheels. They look like they mean business. The business of being mean!

Ivan the Horrible jumps off his horse and squares up to me.

"You are John Smith, the greatest knight in the land," he growls. "But you are no match for Ivan the Horrible!"

Ivan the Horrible takes his glove off and

tosses it on the ground. "I'm throwing down the gauntlet," he laughs.

"And I'm throwing down…" I look around and see an old washing line in the corner of the courtyard. "… a dirty old pair of pants!" I throw the pants on the ground and work them into the grit with my heel.

"Those are my knickers!" says an old washerwoman.

"Sorry about that," I whisper.

Ivan turns to Bruno the Bone Breaker, Thor the Eyeball Sucker and Terry the Toe Tickler and cackles for a very long time. "I'll hand it to you, John Smith, you've got bags of nerve," he roars. "What if I cut you into a thousand pieces and feed you to my horses?"

"Do your worst. We're not scared of you!" I reply.

"I will do my worst," says Ivan. "I will set Terry the Toe Tickler to work on your little tootsies!"

Terry the Toe Tickler wiggles his fingers and guffaws, which sets all the others off guffawing too, a sort of Mexican wave guffaw.

"I am here to sack, loot and pillage!" snarls Ivan. "Which means I will steal your food, burn your castle to the ground and ride off with your queen! Why don't you join my army, John Smith? We'll be a truly terrible team!"

"Never!" I yell. "My place is here. Besides, I already know a truly terrible team – and if you've ever seen United play football, you'll know a truly terrible team too."

"Very well," says Ivan. "Have it your own way." He turns to his revolting gang. "All right, you lot, let's get horrible!"

Bruno the Bone Breaker, Thor the Eyeball Sucker and Terry the Toe Tickler jump down from their horses and move slowly towards me, their hands reaching for their weapons.

Now for the plan.

I pass word round to let our furry little friends work their magic.

Ossie, Egbert and Perkin pluck the mice from their pockets. They sneak round the back of Ivan's no-good, nasty army and drop the mice inside their no-good, nasty suits of armour, finishing up with the fattest, scratchiest mice for Bruno, Thor and Terry.

Bruno the Bone Breaker draws his sword and says: "I am Bruno the Bone Breaker and I've got one thing to say to you..."

He suddenly twists his mouth into a funny shape and goes all bug-eyed.

"It's... It's... Aaaaa... Oooooo..." he gasps.

Bruno begins to dance around in a little circle, flapping his arms. Ivan the Horrible looks at Bruno and shakes his head.

"Bruno, you're letting the side down!" he snarls.

Bruno falls to the ground and rolls round on his back, screaming and raging, "Make it stop!"

Thor the Eyeball Sucker takes a step forward.

"Thor the Eyeball Sucker, do your worst," I holler.

"I am Thor the... Ho ho ho ... ah ... ah ... ah!" he giggles.

Thor joins in with the funny dance, shaking his legs, slapping his thighs, gasping for breath.

Terry the Toe Tickler rushes forward. "This be death by tickling!" he announces. "I have seen it a thousand times."

Terry the Toe Tickler produces a pink feather duster on the end of a very long stick.

"You cannot out-tickle a tickler..." he declares before he too falls into fits of laughter. "Ha! Ha ha ha ... heeeeeee... Stop tickling! STOP TICKLING!"

"It's unbearable!" groans Bruno, trying to unbuckle his breastplate.

"It's intolerable!" cries Thor, rubbing his back against a wall.

"My tickling days are behind me!" wails Terry the Toe Tickler, throwing his tickling stick in the air and hopping hysterically out of the castle gates.

Ivan's army tumble down the hill, stumbling and screaming, scratching and shrieking, before falling into the moat. Everyone in the castle cheers and shouts.

Except for Ivan – he's not happy at all. And he brings out his really big sword and swipes it around his head, menacingly. "Playtime is over!" he growls.

He drops his visor over his face, leaving no gap, not even for the mousiest mouse in the house. "Prepare to die!"

Ivan runs at me, flashing his sword. I bring

up my shield as the blows rain down. "It's the end for you, John Smith!" he roars.

I draw my sword but Ivan smashes it away.

"Is that the best you can do?" he thunders.

He plunges his sword into my shield and rips it out of my hands.

"Now you are defenceless," he rages.

He takes several strides towards me, his sword at the ready.

"I can smell victory," he booms.

He's given me an idea!

I spin sideways and grab Ossie's bow and arrow.

"A bow and arrow?" laughs Ivan. "What match is that for my suit of iron?"

"We'll see about that," I grunt.

I turn to the beggar with the pongy feet.

"One kilo of your finest toe cheese, please."

"Coming up," says the beggar.

He scrapes a rich seam of toe goo on to the arrowhead.

"What is this potion?" says Ivan.

"Why don't you try some for yourself?" I reply.

I draw the arrow back and fire it straight

at Ivan. It zips through the air and wedges
in his visor.

Everyone holds their breath.

Ivan starts to cough and choke. He flaps his arms around, staggers towards me, sneezing and wheezing.

"Oh, the pong, the pongy, PONG, PONG..." he gurgles.

He raises his sword into the air, stands still for a good few seconds ... then comes tumbling down with an almighty crash!

"The smell has knoked him out!" gasps Perkin.

"What are we going to do now?" says Ossie.

"Now we take him and wedge him into the catapult!" I reply. So we gather round and lift him into the sling.

Ivan opens his eyes and looks around.

"What happened?" he groans. "Where am I?"

"Ready to launch!" I holler.

"What are you doing?" he shrieks.

"Chucking out the garbage," I chuckle. "OK, boys, take it away!"

Everyone in the castle joins in with the countdown...

"Three! Two! One!"

Ossie slashes the rope and releases the catapult.

"Waaaaaaaaaaaaaa!!!"

Ivan flies over the castle wall and plunges into the moat. That's definitely the last we'll be seeing of him!

"Three cheers for John Smith!" says Ossie. "For he is the greatest!"

They carry me round the courtyard, chanting my name.

I could get used to this life!

CHAPTER NINE

"You have done well this day, John Smith," says the Queen. "You have seen off Ivan the Horrible. You have freed our people to live in peace and prosperity, and for that we thank you."

"All in a day's work, Your Maj," I grin.

The Queen takes a long shiny sword and asks me to kneel. I think I know what's coming next. It's goodbye, plain old John Smith. From now on they'll be calling me

Sir John the Brave!

"All that is left for me to say," announces the Queen, "is CHOP HIS HEAD OFF!"

The guards close in around me and pull me to my feet. Well, this is a fine thank-you for saving the day! I don't know why I bothered. What is the Queen doing?

"You stole my precious red ruby!" says the Queen.

"I ... what? Not me, Your Majesty," I splutter.

The Queen points at the tapestry on the wall, the one Ossie showed me earlier. "So what do you call this, then?"

I look at the tapestry. I see Ossie and his mum and dad, Egbert, Perkin ... and there in the far corner is a picture of me with my grubby mitts on the Queen's red ruby!

"Do you take me for a complete

blockhead?" she growls. "You are John Smith, aren't you?"

"I'm afraid so," I nod.

"And as you have said yourself," continues the Queen, "you are the only John Smith in the land!"

"But that can't be me!" I protest.

And then the penny drops. Granddad was here a long time ago and it was Granddad who took the Queen's ruby! That's why Granddad didn't want me to go on this adventure! That's why he warned me not to lose my head!

"Off with his head..." says the Queen.

Woodworm the executioner steps forward with his really sharp axe. "My pleasure, Your Majesty," he smiles.

I spring to my feet, run across the courtyard and leap on to Daisy. Everyone is shouting "Come back, John Smith!" or "There he goes – the Special One!"

"I'm not the Special One," I cry. "I'm a totally ordinary little boy. Just leave me alone."

I gallop away, charging through washing lines and splashing through puddles until Daisy rears up and throws me on to the cobblestones. I look up and see Woodworm blocking my way.

"Sorry," says the Queen, "but it's the end of the road for you."

Woodworm slides his finger down the blade of his axe.

"Chop his head off," says the Queen.

Woodworm lifts the axe.

"If you chop his head off," says Ossie, "you'll never get your ruby back!"

The Queen thinks about it for a moment.

"That's true," admits the Queen. "So what do you propose to do about it?"

"We'll return the ruby, Your Majesty," says Ossie. Then he looks at me and nods. "We can do it, can't we, John?"

"Absolutely," I smile, "one hundred per cent. You have my word."

What they don't know is I can escape just by saying the magic words that got me here in the first place.

"To stop you running away, Ossie," warns the Queen, "we'll look after your mother and father."

The guards close in round Ossie's mum and dad. The Queen pats Ossie on the head.

"Do this for me and I promise your mother a lifetime's supply of turnips."

"Thank you, Your Majesty," says Ossie's mum, scraping a curtsy down to the ground.

"But if you *don't* return my ruby," continues the Queen, "we'll throw your parents in a dungeon for a thousand years!"

"And get to work on their tootsies!" sneers Woodworm, holding up Terry the Toe Tickler's tickling stick.

Oh dear, now there is no escape. I have to get the ruby back to the Queen.

"You have one hour to return my ruby!" she says.

"It's a deal!" I reply. "Come on, Ossie, let's go."

We walk out of the castle gate and over the drawbridge.

"Where now?" says Ossie.

"Now, we're going to a strange land, far,

far away..." I smile.

At least I hope we're going to a strange land far, far away. I haven't got a clue whether I can take Ossie back with me. Only one way to find out.

I hold Ossie's hand as I speak the magic words...

"Say it long, say it loud – I'm JOHN SMITH and I'm proud!"

CHAPTER TEN

"What is this land of miracles?" gasps Ossie.

"This is my granddad's bedroom," I reply.

I'm surprised to find that I'm still in my knight's costume.

"It is a most marvellous place," says Ossie. "Filled with many wonders!" Ossie lifts Granddad's dentures out of a glass by the side of the bed. "Maybe we should ask this magical talking mouth where we can find the ruby…"

At that moment Granddad walks into the room.

"Maybe we should just ask my granddad," I reply. "That's why you didn't want me to be a knight in armour, Granddad, because you stole the Queen's red ruby!"

"I didn't steal the Queen's ruby," says Granddad. "I thought it was a present for

defeating Norman the Norman – and that's a whole other story!"

"I nearly got my head chopped off," I frown.

"I'm sorry about that," sighs Granddad.

"We need to get the ruby back to the Queen," says Ossie.

"Mmmm," says Granddad, "that might be a bit of a problem. Your sister has borrowed the ruby, John!"

"Well, I'll turn her room upside down until I find it!" I protest.

"The trouble is, the ruby's not in her room," replies Granddad.

"Where is it, Granddad?" I scowl.

"She's wearing it in the school play!" murmurs Granddad.

"What?" I gasp. "I've got to get it back to the Queen!"

"Then you'd better get your skates on," says Granddad. "The show's about to start!"

CHAPTER ELEVEN

"That's Hayley in the middle of the stage," I whisper.

Picture the scene: I'm shuffling along a beam which is over the stage in Hayley's school – her BIG SCHOOL. A few feet below me, Hayley is singing her heart out in the school musical with Rufus. Around Hayley's neck is the Queen's fat red ruby! As you can see, it's all very dramatic...

I take a deep breath.

"We mess this up, Ossie, and they're going to put my head on a spike, bury me alive and feed me to the birds!" I gulp.

"Understood," says Ossie. "I think..."

Hayley and Rufus are in the middle of a cheesy song.

"What do you reckon, Ossie?"

"It's going to be a brilliant success," says Ossie.

"You really think so?"

"Just listen to that lovely singing!" he sighs.

"Not the musical! What do you reckon of our chances?"

"Ooh," Ossie scrunches his nose. "For a normal boy this would be a disaster. But for you, John Smith, anything is possible."

Ossie looks at me and winks.

"Hold my ankles, Ossie..." I grunt.

This is a very tricky situation. Hayley is about to do a girly, yucky, gooey, kissy-kissy snogathon with Rufus who already totally hates my guts. And I'm about to drop on the stage and spoil the show.

"After we're done here – meet me back at the house," I whisper.

"Good luck," says Ossie, "and remember – your people love you..."

Here's my plan: when Hayley kisses Rufus, the lights will go down. Before the lights come up again, I will drop in the darkness and snatch the ruby from around my sister's neck.

That is the plan.

This is what happens.

Ossie lowers me down a bit too quickly, and I plunge upside down between my sister and Rufus in view of the audience, but they've both got their eyes closed, which is what people do when they're about to kiss and what you should *definitely* do if

you're about to kiss my sister because she looks like a camel.

So Rufus is moving in for the kill but instead of kissing my sister he kisses me, ON THE LIPS, on stage, in front of the headmaster, the teachers, a reporter from the local newspaper, Mum and Dad and five hundred other mums and dads at Cherry Tree School.

Everyone is extremely shocked. I am extremely shocked. Ossie is extremely shocked. And he puts his hands to his face and cries out "No!!!!!" which means he's not holding my ankles. Which means I drop directly on top of my sister and she rolls over with her feet in the air and her knickers on show.

Everyone falls about laughing.

Rufus stares at me, his face all mean and twisted.

"YOU … YOU … YOU!!!"

He jumps at me, slips on Hayley's skirt, falls off the edge of the stage and crashes into the orchestra.

I grab the ruby and run through the audience. The headmaster kicks his chair

away and shouts, "Stop that boy!" and the chase is on. The mums, dads and teachers of Cherry Tree School are coming after me!

I run out of the school and into the playground. Oh no, they've locked the school gates. . .

"Give it up," says the headmaster.

Everyone makes a big circle all around me. There's no way I'm getting the ruby back to the Queen now. Ossie's mum and dad are getting their feet tickled for a thousand years!

Then I get an idea.

I see a big wheelie bin at the top of the playground. I'll ride it into the school gates as fast as I can. I'm going to smash my way to freedom.

I leap on to the bin. Next stop home!

CRUNCH!!!

The bin bashes through the school gates. Everything in the bin goes flying in the air.

I get a face full of rotting bones, smelly veg and dirty disgusting bin juice.

I wipe the slime from my eyes and pick a kipper from my mouth.

"Until we meet again," I announce.

I steer the bin down the hill and towards my house.

"I'll get you, John Smith!" screams Hayley.

I ride the bin across town, jump free at the garden gate, sprint up the path, through the front door and belt up the stairs.

Ossie is sitting on Granddad's bed, waiting for me.

"The Queen's ruby!" I gasp.

Ossie takes the brilliant red gem and slides it into his pocket.

"Farewell, John Smith," he smiles. "This has been a brilliant adventure."

"Before you go, I want to say something," I mutter. "About my name — it isn't special or rare. The truth is, John Smith is the most common name in the world. It's like my mum says – I'm one in a million..."

Ossie looks at me in a really weird way. "Your mum says you're one in a million?"

"I'm afraid so," I shrug.

"You know, for a smart boy, you can be a bit of a tickle-brain!" he laughs. "Maybe your mum means you're one in a million *to her*!"

"Oh, right," I reply.

I still don't know what he's going on about.

I hear Hayley leading the charge up the road. I'm running out of time.

"Get this ruby back to the Queen..." I whisper.

"I'll make sure it's done," says Ossie. "Goodbye, Sir John Smith..."

"Goodbye, Oswald Periwinkle," I reply.

Then we both burst out laughing.

The bit after everything has happened...

I write a letter to the headmaster pretending to be someone in the audience saying the whole show had been a brilliant stunt and well done Cherry Tree School for an evening of unexpected entertainment. The headmaster has no choice but to agree and the matter is quietly dropped.

Show and Tell is the best ever because I draw my own comic strip with the whole story in cartoons from beginning to end and I show the class my drawing and tell them this incredible story – about this really ordinary boy with this extraordinary life who went into battle as a knight in shining armour, and do you think anyone believes me? Of course they don't! After all ... I'm JOHN SMITH.

But *you* know, don't you.

Have you read John Smith's other

NOT BORING!

adventures?

John Smith is NOT BORING!

CAP'N John THE (SLIGHTLY) FIERCE

by Johnny Smith

"I expect you'll want to prepare yourself for the bloody skirmish that is about to follow," says the pirate with the banana bandana, walking with me to what looks like the captain's cabin.

"Oh yes," I chuckle. "I can't wait to get my hands on that Captain Black. Why, I'll kick him in the shin and give him a Chinese burn…"

"And kill him?" says the pirate with the banana bandana.

"You betcha!" I nod.

"And keelhaul him?" he grunts.

"Absolutely. I'll keelhaul him like a good 'un," I reply. "What again, just remind me, is keelhauling?"

"Simple, Captain," he smiles. "You tie a man on to a piece of rope, throw him in the water and drag him under the ship, where the barnacles scrape his belly to bits."

That is a very strange party game! Still, it beats blind man's bluff or stick the tail on the donkey any day of the week.

"I'll man the lookout," says the pirate with the banana bandana. "Will you be wanting your usual pre-skirmish meal, Cap'n?"

"Uh, yes," I reply. "Bring me my usual – and plenty of it!"

I make myself at home in my captain's cabin. It's a brilliant place. There are maps and globes, lots of curly swords on the walls, and best of all ... a hammock!

Where is Hector? I hope he's having as much fun as me.

I go to the porthole and pull aside the little curtain.

"AAAAAHHHH!!!"

Who is that mean and wicked pirate staring back at me, a funny three-pointed hat on his head and a natty blue-and-yellow scarf round his throat?

Oh, it's me! It's just my reflection.

"I am Cap'n John the Fierce and I'll have you lot for breakfast," I growl.

I grab a sword off the wall and dance round the cabin, saying things like "Shiver me timbers!" even though I've got no idea what me timbers are or why they're shivering.

I launch myself into the hammock, bounce

out of the netting, splat into the wall and plop on the floor.

"Everything all right, Captain?" says Peg Leg Reg, hobbling through the door with a large pot on a silver tray.

"Oh yes," I reply. "Just trying out the old hammock."

"Nice one, Captain," he cackles. "Anyway, here you go, the captain's lunch!"

Peg Leg Reg pulls the top off the pot.

"Live eels, Cap'n. Your favourite food

before a battle."

Oh dear, the plate is a moving mass of massive worms.

"Put them on the side, Reg. I'll have them later," I groan.

He moves a bit closer and darts his shifty eyes around to make sure no one's listening. "If you don't mind me asking, Captain, but any chance I can see your snarl?"

"My what?" I reply.

"You know, your horribly twisted face," he grunts. "Only, I've followed you into battle many a time, but never got to see your snarl up close…"

"Oh, my snarl? Yes, it's an excellent snarl, one of the best," I chuckle. "Did you know I was snarling champion two years running?"

"Is that a fact?" he replies. "Go on then, just between you and me – show us your snarl."

I twist my face and mouth into a really

mean growl.

Peg Leg Reg stares at me.
"That's your snarl?"

Oh dear, I think my
snarling powers aren't up
to much. I wasn't really
snarling champion; I
was just trying to play
my part.

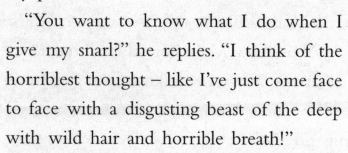

"You want to know what I do when I
give my snarl?" he replies. "I think of the
horriblest thought – like I've just come face
to face with a disgusting beast of the deep
with wild hair and horrible breath!"

So I think of Hayley first thing in the
morning.

"Oh, that is a superb snarl!" he says. "They
don't call you Cap'n John the Fierce for
nothing."

He's right about that. They don't call me

Cap'n John the Fierce at all. They call me John Smith, and some other names I can't tell you about. But this is much better.

I could really get to love being a pirate. I never knew there was so much to it. It's not all about saying "Aaaargh", you know. You get to say "Oooooh-aaaaargh" quite a lot too. And you get to gnarl and gnash your teeth and run round on the deck of the ship swishing your sword. There's a lot of swishing, I can tell you.

It is a brilliant life being a pirate.

TO BE CONTINUED...

Other

NOT
BORING!

adventures from

John Smith

Johnny Smith is an experienced animation and live-action screenwriter. As one half of Sprackling and Smith, the comedy screenwriting team, he sold numerous original feature film scripts here and in Hollywood, including Disney's box office hit GNOMEO & JULIET. He lives in London with his wife and children.